I CAN EAT A RAINBOW

This Book Belongs To:

_____

To Sagen, the best storyteller I know!

chicken nuggets and mac and cheese: I want it all. I am begging, please.

I want some ice cream and some candy. I will have some cake if it is handy.

But first, I must eat my fruit and veggies before I get to eat my spaghetti.

I will eat some greens. I will eat some beans.

I will eat some berries. I will eat some cherries.

It won't take me long. I will grow big and strong.

I will have energy to play, each and every day.

I can add some fruit in my yogurt for a snack. Or I can eat some veggies that my Mommy packed.

Eating colorful fruits and veggies is good for my brain, just like reading or playing with my trains.

Tomato

Orange

Carrot

Banana

Mushroom

Try to fill half your plate with fruits and vegetables every day!

Pineapple

Grapes

Apple

Broccoli

Corn

If I want to stay healthy and well, I will make sure to eat a serving of veggies with...mmm, what is that smell?

The End

COLOR YOUR OWN RAINBOW

Made in the USA
Middletown, DE
11 July 2023